PHARRELL WILLIAMS

G. P. PUTNAM'S SONS

G. P. Putnam's Sons
an imprint of Penguin Random House LLC
375 Hudson Street
New York, NY 10014

Library of Congress Cataloging-in-Publication Data is available upon request.

Printed in the United States of America
ISBN 978-0-399-17643-2
1 3 5 7 9 10 8 6 4 2

Interior photography by Amanda Pratt.

Design and photo illustrations by Kristin Smith.
Props created by Andi Burnett.
Wardrobe styling by Michel Onofrio.
Additional photographs courtesy of Shutterstock.com.
Text set in Gotham.

To Rocket and all his friends.

Thank you for teaching me
to see the world in a new light.

It might seem

CRAZY

what I'm about to SAY!

SUNSHINE

she's here,

you can take

a break.

I'm a

HOT

AIR

BALLOON

that could go to
SPACE.

With the air like

I DON'T
CARE,

baby,
by
the way.

Because I'm
HAPPY!

Clap along
if you feel
like a room
without a
ROOF.

Because I'm **HAPPY!**

Clap along
if you feel
like happiness
is the
TRUTH.

Because I'm **HAPPY!**

Clap along if you know what happiness is to **YOU.**

Because I'm HAPPY!

Clap along if you feel like
that's what you wanna **DO.**

Here
comes
BAD NEWS

talking **THIS**
and
THAT.

Well, gimme ALL you GOT and don't HOLD BACK.

Well, I should probably **WARN** you, I'll be **JUST FINE.**

Because I'm **HAPPY!**

Clap along if you feel like a room without a ROOF.

Because I'm **HAPPY!**

Clap along if you know what happiness is to YOU.

Because I'm HAPPY!

Clap along if you feel like that's what you wanna DO.

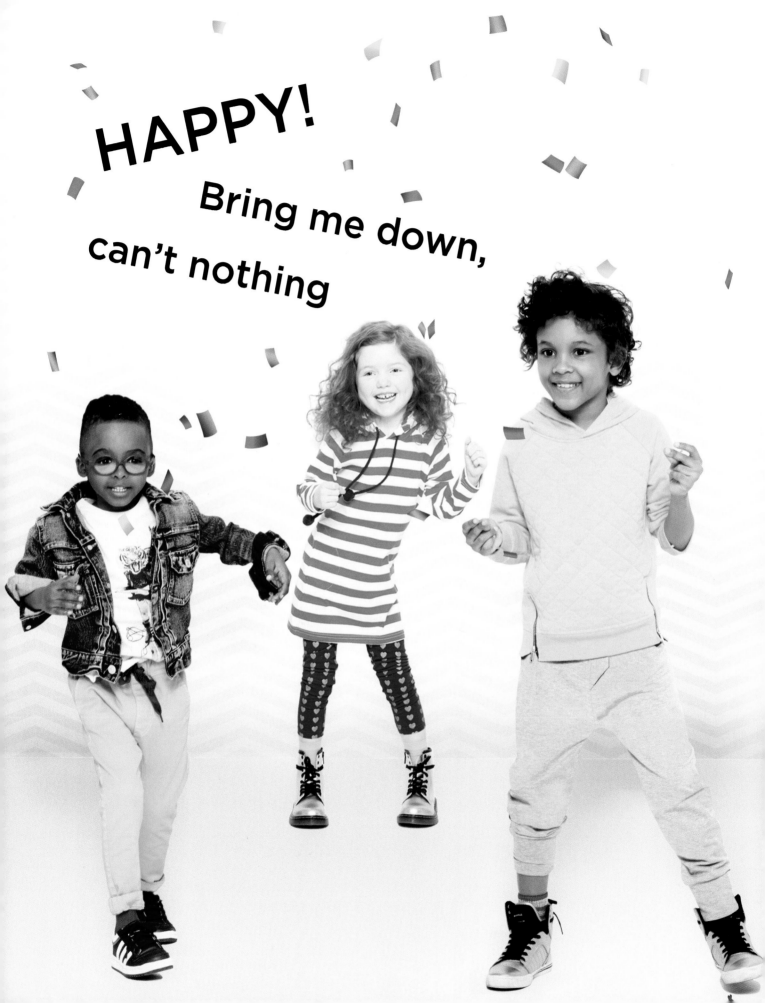

HAPPY!
Bring me down,
can't nothing

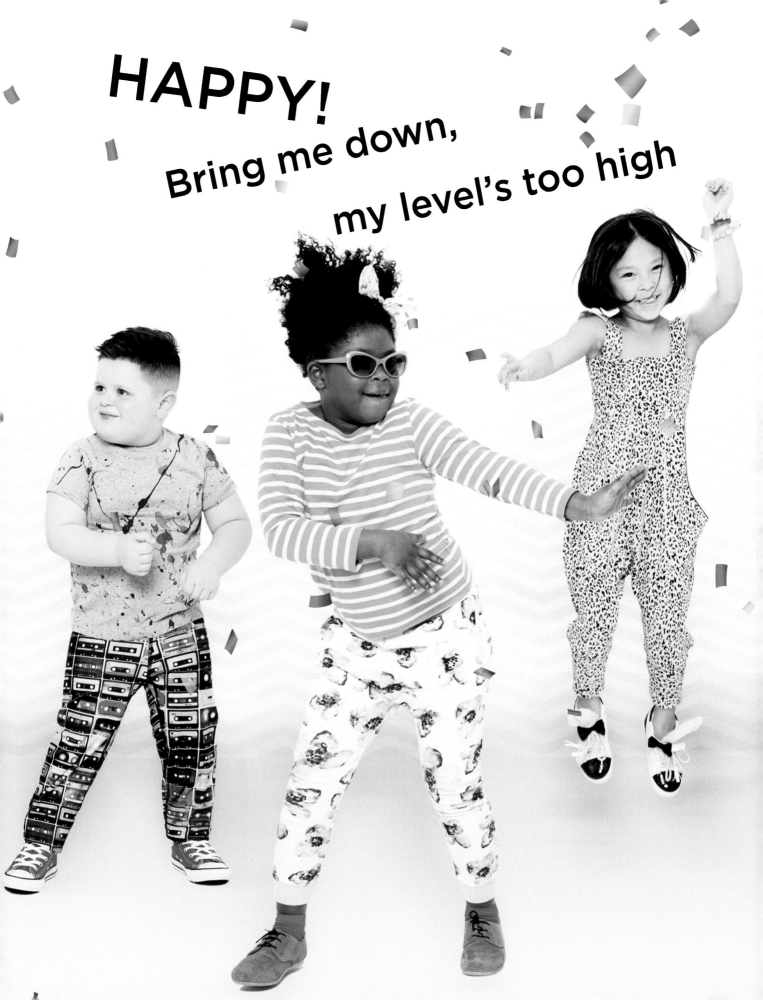

HAPPY!
Bring me down,
my level's too high

HAPPY!

Bring me down,
can't nothing

HAPPY!

Bring me down.

Dear Friend,

You're awesome. Yes, you!

If you had fun reading my book, then that means you're a Happy Helper! What is that, you say? Well, I'm really glad you asked.

A Happy Helper has a very important job in the world. We love our family and friends so much, we want to make them smile all the time. It's cool to bring happiness to someone's day. Does that sound like something you like to do? I knew it!

Everyone knows how to do something that makes people happy. When I was little, I discovered I could make others smile by creating music. Happiness can lift your mood, and the right song can help do that perfectly. I hope that every time you hear the song "Happy" (from Despicable Me 2), you dance like no one's watching, smile like love, and believe that happiness can change the world.

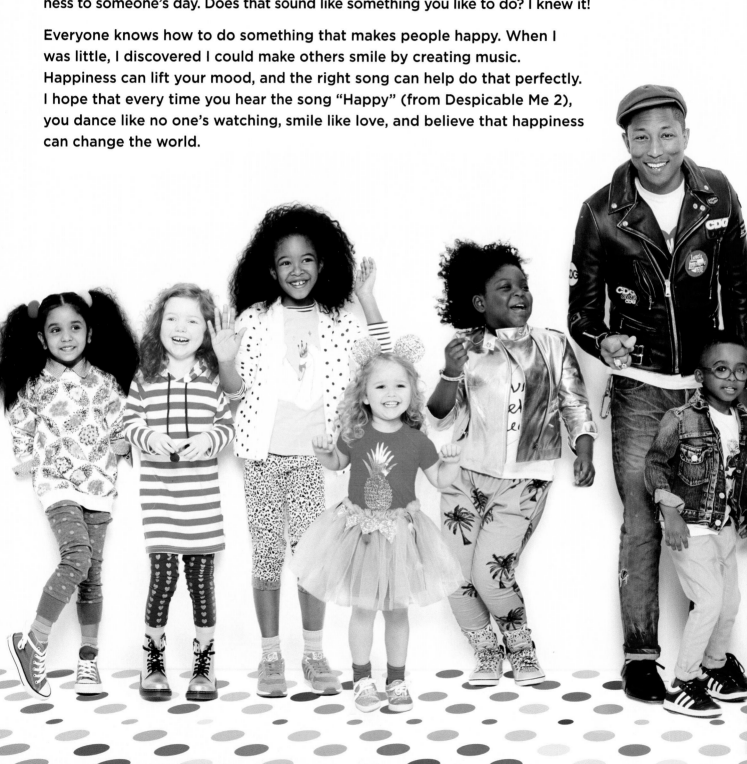

How do you feel when you make someone smile? It's the best feeling ever, right? I believe it's everyone's responsibility to bring more laughter into the world. Use your imagination to figure out new ways to make others smile. Let's never forget that happiness is contagious! There isn't a day that goes by where I don't appreciate the beauty of a smile. It's pretty obvious every human being on the planet needs to feel happy. Don't you agree?

Okay, so here's what I would like for you to do. If you're a Happy Helper and you enjoyed this book, then pass it along. I'm counting on you to spread happiness and make lots of people smile today!

Are you ready? Go!

In service,
Pharrell